For Norman and Daniel, with love

LADYBIRD BOOKS, INC.
Auburn, Maine 04210 U.S.A.
© LADYBIRD BOOKS LTD 1989
Loughborough, Leicestershire, England

Printed in England

Marcus and Lionel

By Ronne P. Randall
Illustrated by Joe Ewers

Ladybird Books

Marcus and Lionel had
been together for as long as they
could remember. They lived on the
little girl's bed, propped up against her pillows.

Marcus often went places with the little girl. And when he got home, he always told Lionel about his adventures. Lionel was too big to travel, and never got to go anywhere. Sometimes he wished he could have an adventure of his own, but most of the time he was content to sit on the bed and hear about the world outside.

One summer morning, there was lots of bustle and clatter in the house. People had come with boxes to pack things in, and there was a van to take everything away. The little girl and her parents were moving to the country.

Marcus was going to ride in the car. But Lionel was packed in a box, along with the pillows and some blankets. He just had time to say good-by to Marcus before the lid was closed.

Marcus had a wonderful journey. There was so much to see!
They rode through busy city streets, one after the other. Then
they came to a big bridge. Marcus had never seen a bridge
before. "Wait till I tell Lionel about this!" he thought.

As they crossed the bridge, Marcus saw boats sailing. When they got to the other side, he saw hills and a windmill and cows in a field.

"I can't wait to tell Lionel!" Marcus thought.

At last they arrived at the new house. There was a porch at the front, and swings and a slide in the yard. The little girl's room looked out over a garden with red roses growing in it.

"Lionel and I will be happy here," Marcus thought.

The little girl and her parents started to unpack
the boxes. Marcus could hardly wait to see Lionel.

They unpacked the little girl's clothes, and all her books. They unpacked her dollhouse and her cowboy hat and boots. There was no sign of Lionel yet.

They unpacked the tea set, the easel, and the bedside lamp. There was still no sign of Lionel.

There was only one box left. "Lionel has to be in that one,"
Marcus thought.

But he wasn't. It was only the little girl's record player and
records.

That night, the little girl had to sleep with her mother's pillow —and no Lionel. She hugged Marcus extra tight, and Marcus tried hard to hug her back. "I'm *sure* Lionel will turn up," he thought.

But Lionel didn't.

Over the next few days, Marcus and the little girl had lots of new things to explore. There were trees to climb at the back of the house, and a little stream with frogs and fish. There was a hidey-hole under the porch, and there were four cats next door who came to visit.

Discovering it all should have been a great adventure, but it wasn't much fun for Marcus. Lionel wasn't there to hear about it when he came home. The days seemed very long.

One day, the little girl took Marcus out to the car. She and her mother were going to visit someone in the city, and Marcus was going, too.

On the way, Marcus saw lots of things he remembered from the moving day. That made him miss Lionel more than ever.

When they got to the city, the little girl carried Marcus in her usual way, by one arm. This always gave Marcus an interesting view of things.

And that day Marcus got a *very* interesting view of something. Behind an iron fence, on the lawn in front of a big gray building, there were all sorts of things set out on display. Chairs, and clothes, and clocks, and tables filled with books...

And there, on one of those tables, was—could it be?
Yes! It was Lionel!

Marcus had to make the little girl stop, so she would see Lionel, too. But how? She and her mother seemed to be in such a hurry!

There was only one way. Gathering all his strength, Marcus stuck out one leg—just far enough to get his foot caught in the fence.

As the little girl walked on, Marcus's foot began to tear. It hurt terribly. But it would be worth it, if only...

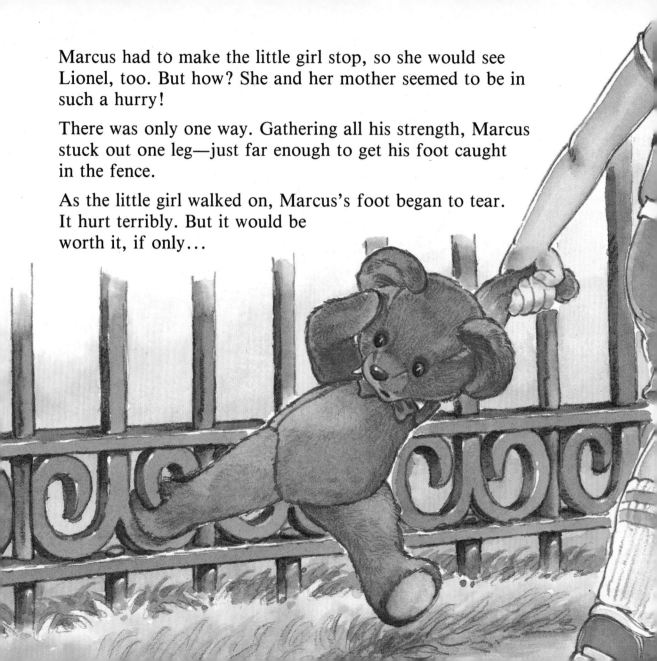

"Mama, wait," said the little girl, stopping. "Marcus's foot is stuck."

As the little girl began to free his foot, she suddenly saw what Marcus had seen.

"Mama!" she cried. "Mama, look! It's Lionel! We found him, Mama!"

Indeed they had. He was a bit dusty, and one of his seams was
torn, but otherwise he was fine. They got him from the
rummage sale, and that afternoon they took him home to the
country. The little girl's mother fixed his seam and gave him a
bath. She fixed Marcus's foot, too, so it didn't hurt any more.

Marcus and Lionel were so happy to be together again. They spent days and days catching up on all that had happened. It was just like old times. Well, almost: now Lionel had adventures to tell Marcus about, too!